MAX CHASE

BLOOMSBURY

LONDON BERLIN NEW YORK SYDNEY

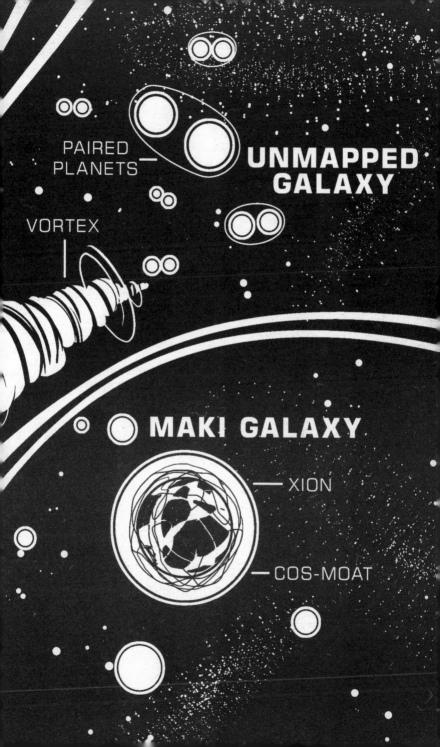

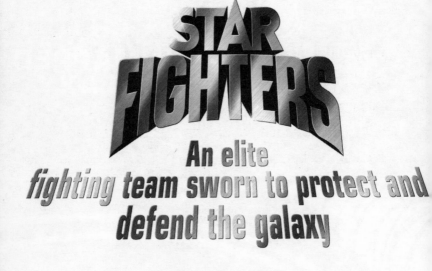

STAR FIGHTERS

An elite *fighting team sworn to protect and defend the galaxy*

It is the year 5012 and the Milky Way galaxy is under attack . . .

After the Universal War . . . a war that almost brought about the destruction of every known universe . . . the planets in the Milky Way banded together to create the Intergalactic Force – an elite fighting team sworn to protect and defend the galaxy.

Only the brightest and most promising students are accepted into the Intergalactic Force Academy, and only the very best cadets reach the highest of their ranks and become . . .

To be a Star Fighter is to dedicate your life to one mission: *Peace in Space*. They are given the coolest weapons, the fastest spaceships – and the most dangerous missions. Everyone at the Intergalactic Force Academy wants to be a Star Fighter someday.

Do YOU have what it takes?

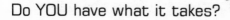

Chapter 1

'Follow that ship,' Prince Onix screamed across the Bridge of the *Phoenix*. He pointed at the Meigwor viper-ship snaking away from the dusty orange planet. 'Make them pay for attacking Xion!'

Peri pulled the thruster levers hard. The *Phoenix* raced after the enemy craft.

'Locking target trackers,' Diesel shouted. The half-Martian gunner cracked his knuckles. 'One X-plode detonator coming up.' He reached for the button on the gunnery station.

1

'Wait a nanosecond, Diesel,' Peri ordered. 'Why is that vipership leaving Xion? Where's the rest of the Meigwor fleet?'

'Who cares?' Diesel replied. 'You blast first and ask questions later.'

'Stop arguing and do something,' the prince snapped. 'You promised my father you'd destroy the Meigwors.'

Peri glared at him. 'We said we'd help save Xion as long as you never attack the Milky Way again. We need to find out what the Meigwors are up to — *then* we can start kicking some alien space-butts.'

'Watch out!' Diesel shouted as alarms erupted across the Bridge.

A huge purple and silver meteorite was plummeting towards them. Peri jerked the Nav-wheel sharply and slammed on the dodge mechanism. The *Phoenix* flew past it.

'What the *prrrip'chiq* was that?' Diesel asked.

'The s-s-space h-h-highway,' stammered Prince Onix. 'Look what the Meigwors have done.'

The twisty, twelve-hundred-lane space highway that had surrounded Xion had been shattered into gazillions of pieces. Huge chunks of Astrophalt were caught in orbit around the planet. The vipership started blasting its way through the debris.

Peri was not going to let it get away. He checked the *Phoenix*'s cloak and activated the sprint-thrusters. The ship zoomed along in the vipership's trail, through the space-carnage.

'The Cos-Moat will slow them down,' Prince Onix said.

'I don't think so,' said Diesel. 'Look!'

The dark blue bubble of corrosive goo that surrounded the whole planet was also in tatters. The viper slithered easily through a gap, with the *Phoenix* close behind.

'We're in their slipstream,' Peri said. 'Next stop the Meigwor fleet!'

Otto's massive bulk and freakishly long neck loomed over Peri. 'Wait! Stop!' he boomed. The Meigwor bounty hunter was part of their crew now, but he hated fighting against his own people. 'We can't defeat the entire fleet! We'll be captured! They'll send me down the mines for being a traitor!'

Peri shook his head. Too much was

riding on this mission. If they stopped the Meigwors, then the king of Xion had promised to send the *Phoenix* back to the Milky Way and never attack their home again.

'No more running away,' Peri said. 'This time we're taking it to the Meigwors. We're going to end this intergalactic conflict and get home. Otto, help Diesel on weapons!'

The bounty hunter shuffled over to the gunnery station. Diesel activated rows of triggers and armed the X-plode detonators.

Tsack! Selene materialised in the empty chair next to Peri.

'Where have you been?' Peri asked.

'Engineering,' Selene replied, wiping a smudge of grease from her cheek. 'I've made an adjustment to boost the emergency thrusters and reconfigured the vaporising lasers.'

'We're going to need all the help we can get,' he replied. Their radiation gauges screeched as the enemy vessel tested its weapons systems. But the viper-ship showed no sign of changing course. The Meigwor vessel hadn't noticed the *Phoenix* shadowing it.

Prince Onix came up beside Peri's chair. Peri almost gagged at the stench of space-squid sweat that came with the prince. 'We've got to do something!' Onix said.

'It's no use!' Otto boomed. 'The entire fleet of vipers will swoop down on Xion and your cowardly people will surrender! They'll be slaves to the victorious Meigwors before the day is done!'

'Otto!' Peri and Selene scolded.

'What?' Otto demanded, then laughed. 'Our entire fleet is attacking Xion! You think this puny ship can stop them?'

The viper-ship banked suddenly. Peri slammed on the steering-thrusters. He steered hard, following the craft towards the dark side of the planet.

As the glare from the sun vanished, Peri's jaw dropped. Instead of viper-ships lined up for attack, he saw a huge black cylinder like a gigantic, armour-plated Saturn Soda can. It was orbiting Xion slowly. Peri felt a cold shiver through his circuits.

The viper-ship stopped and another pulled alongside. Tentacles sprang from the second craft and latched on to the first one. The two ships locked together like a jigsaw puzzle. More thin tentacles then lashed the vessels into a massive cylindrical mega-hull. *There has to be more than a thousand ships already in the mega-cylinder*, Peri thought. *And hundreds more are joining it.*

Whatever it was, Peri knew it had to be bad news for Xion. The Meigwors had created some sort of unspeakable weapon. And Otto was right. There was not a space-puppy's chance in a meteorite storm that the *Phoenix* could destroy it alone.

Peri leapt from his chair. 'What is that thing?' He grabbed Otto by the lumps on his long neck. 'Why didn't you warn us?'

Otto's face had lost the smirk. The black patches around his eyes had shrunk in absolute terror as he stared at the mega-cylinder. 'I didn't know,' he said. 'I can't believe it . . . It *does* exist.' He seemed genuinely shocked at what they were seeing.

Peri could feel the Meigwor's muscular body trembling. 'Otto, talk to us!' he said.

'It's not possible,' Otto gasped. 'The Extractor . . . It's a myth. It's not real . . .

It's just a story to scare primitive species! But . . . But . . . There it is!'

'Just tell us what an Extractor *does!*' Peri yelled at Otto.

Otto shivered and took a deep breath. 'You don't understand! The Extractor is the ultimate piece of Meigwor technology! It can completely drain a planet of carbon dioxide and then store it! But . . .'

'But what?' Peri pressed.

'The force of the extraction will make the planet implode!' Otto replied. 'The Meigwors have talked about it for more than a hundred years, but I didn't know we'd constructed one for real!'

'Something's happening,' Selene shouted.

Peri looked out through the monitor. A hatch opened from the base of the Extractor. A massive tentacle whipped through the Cos-Moat as if it was nothing more than jelly. It latched on to the Xion atmosphere with suction cups the size of the Earth's Moon.

Chhuuunnhhhuuunnnhhh! A deafening hum rattled the atmosphere like a mega-turbo engine. Green light pulsed down the tentacle towards the planet. Comet-sized bubbles boiled up the tentacle's skin as carbon dioxide was pumped into the Extractor.

'We should run,' Diesel said. 'Get out of here before the planet implodes.'

'The space-monkey's right,' Otto said.

'I hate agreeing with either of them,' Selene said. 'But the Meigwors will vaporise us before we even make a dent in the armour-plating.'

'You're giving up?' Prince Onix shouted. 'Look at my planet! All those innocent people! If it was your home, wouldn't you try *anything* to save it?'

Peri stared at the pulsing tentacle. The Extractor was the most terrifying thing he'd ever seen. But he knew he couldn't run away

'Listen,' he said. 'At the Intergalactic Force Academy we're taught to do the right thing. We're going to help save Xion – even if we have to risk our lives to do it!'

Chapter 2

Peri's hands darted over the control panel, selecting the Exo-Scanner to get a closer look at the Extractor. A 3-D holographic projection of the monstrous ship appeared in front of him. Even at a greatly reduced scale, the Extractor was ridiculously big.

And it was *growing*.

Viper-ships were still flocking towards it and locking on to the weapon's massive hall. But that wasn't the only problem. The Exo-Scanner could not see inside the vessel. Peri knew what this meant. The radioactive armour-plating was so thick, even the X-cite detonators wouldn't be able to penetrate it.

As if reading his mind, Otto boomed, 'This is crazy! Every viper is loaded with ultracombat craft! As soon as you fire, it'll be like flying into an astro-wasps' nest! You'll be obliterated in seconds!'

Anger built up inside Peri like static electricity. It was as if the Extractor had sucked out all the good ideas from his brain. He slammed his palm against the control panel in frustration.

'Everyone think!' he shouted. 'The Extractor must have a weak point. Everything has *one* weak spot.'

'We could try to hack into their computer systems,' Selene exclaimed. She flipped a control panel to reveal a touch-screen keyboard and started typing. She stopped suddenly. 'It's no good – their cyber-defences are too strong. We'll never get inside the system this way.'

'Inside the system!' Peri exclaimed. 'Remember how we defeated the Xio-Bot? We found a way to crawl inside its brain and rip out its circuits.'

'Crazy space-monkeys!' Otto boomed. 'The Extractor's nothing like a Xio-Bot. For a start, it hasn't got a brain, it's a ship!'

'Forget the brain part,' Peri said. 'We just need to get inside the Extractor and find the nerve centre which controls the whole weapon – then we can figure out how to destroy it.'

'You make it sound easy,' Diesel scoffed. 'I don't remember being taught how to sneak aboard enemy ships back at the Academy. I mean, not that I need lessons, but how do you think we can get aboard *that*? Through the front door?'

Peri glared at Diesel. 'It's got to have vents or something like that,' he said, 'otherwise it would overheat. It can't be completely sealed, right?'

Selene punched some buttons and started zooming into the 3-D hologram to show larger areas of the ship. She scanned along the vessel's armour-plated surface. 'Ah-ha!' she said. 'Look here, a ventilation shaft at the base of the cylindrical hub.' She paused. 'Oh, but it's too small for the *Phoenix*.'

Peri peered closer at the hologram. 'There are space-rafts and life-pods on the *Phoenix*. We could adapt them into attack-pods.'

Selene pressed a button next to the touch screen. As she scrolled through the entries, she read out. 'Pods . . . A-pods, pod-beetle-repellent, expansion pods, Expedition Wear survival pods, J-pods, K-pods, medical pods, mini-pods –'

'Wait,' Peri interrupted. 'What are mini-pods?'

'"*Mini-pods*,"' read Selene. '"*One-person craft designed to fly short distances, limited weapon capacity.*" That's what we need.'

Peri's fingers tingled as he stretched over the control panel. 'I think I can take it from here.' He closed his eyes and listened to his instincts. He was part bionic, built to interface with the *Phoenix*. His fingers twitched over a striped dial. He twisted it five times and gave it a good thump.

Whooooooooooosh!

Five long silver tubes extended out from the *Phoenix*'s hull. The ends swelled until, finally, *pop!* Five egg-shaped pods appeared. Each was a miniature version of the *Phoenix*. Five portals rose under the 360-monitor, glowing yellow.

'*Ch'açh*,' Diesel said. The band of hair across his head spiked with excitement.

With a whirl, mechanical arms swooped down and pushed the ship's crew into their Expedition Wear. Another set of arms strapped double-barrel blasters to everyone's hips, apart from Otto's. The Meigwor had ammo-belts criss-crossing his chest, and five different kinds of weapons tucked into his snakeskin belt.

Diesel pressed a button on the gunnery station and a pack of Eterni-chew gum dropped into his pocket. Peri looked at him, puzzled. The half-Martian grinned. 'Remember last time? That Meigwor vessel reeked worse than an unwashed Xion.'

'To the pods!' Peri said, grabbing a pack of Eterni-chew for himself.

Diesel, Selene and Prince Onix rushed across the Bridge towards the portals. Peri looked back. Otto was completely still, his extra-long arms folded across his chest.

'First of all,' the Meigwor boomed, 'you'll get me killed or captured! Second, you will never succeed!'

'Fine,' Diesel snapped. 'We don't need you anyway.'

'Shut up, Diesel,' Peri yelled. 'We do need him. The Extractor is going to be well guarded. Otto is not only a fierce fighter, but he knows how the Meigwors think.'

Otto didn't budge. Peri clicked his fingers. '*Phoenix*, show us satellite images of Xion.'

The dusty orange streets of Xion appeared across the 360-monitor. In the sky, a huge tentacle was sucking in air and whipping up twisters of dust. People were screaming and running in terror. Parents were trying to stop their children being pulled up by the wind. Peri magnified one family, the two kids were gasping for air. Their skin had started to turn a pale blue. It wouldn't be long before they suffocated.

Prince Onix couldn't bear to watch. He covered his eyes.

'Look at it, Otto,' Peri ordered. 'What did these children do to the mighty Meigwors? Nothing. But the Extractor's killing them anyway.'

Otto's beady eyes didn't even blink. Peri started to worry that the Meigwor might be heartless after all. Peri continued, 'If we don't act now to stop it, the planet will implode.'

After a long moment, Otto started to move towards the portal. 'I will help,' he muttered. 'The Extractor is a cowardly weapon. Not the true way of the Meigwors. Xion should be crushed in a *fair* fight – not like this.'

They ran to the portals. Peri jumped feet first down one of the frictionless tubes. He

zipped through in seconds and dropped into his own mini-pod with a *huurrupt*. As an astro-harness snaked around him, the pod's shell turned transparent. He had a 360-degree view of space.

A control panel slipped below his hands and an earpiece sprang from his collar and slotted in his ear. 'Can you hear me?' he asked.

'Loud and clear,' Selene replied. 'The *Phoenix* will hover here and remain cloaked but it can only cloak our pods for two minutes. Once we detach from the ship, we must get inside the Extractor before the cloak stops working.'

'W-w-what if we d-d-on't?' Prince Onix asked.

'The Meigwors will destroy us first, and then planet Xion.' Peri wiped the sweat from his hands and studied the small radar screen in the control panel. 'Everyone follow me, V-formation. We fly full throttle to the ventilation grate. I'll blow off the cover, then we all dive into the shaft and land. Understood?'

'Bring it on!' Diesel shouted.

Peri took a deep breath. 'Launch in three, two, one . . . *Go!*'

Chapter 3

Peri's pod hurtled through space faster than a shooting star. He moved his Nav-wheel left and right, dodging and swooping around the enemy craft flocking to the Extractor. His crew kept in perfect V-formation behind him.

Another Meigwor viper-ship swung in front of him. The two massive red eye-like scanners stared past the mini-pods without blinking. The *Phoenix*'s limited cloak was still working.

Peri pulled the Nav-wheel hard,

sending his pod close over the twisting segments of another viper-ship. He checked the radar screen, seeing that his crew was matching his course without hesitation. He heard Selene's voice, faint and crackly over the radio: 'One minute fifteen seconds of cloak left.'

Beeeaakkk. Beeeeaak. The collision alarm sounded. Another Meigwor vessel was smashing towards them from the right. Peri slammed on the boosters and his pod surged forward. G-forces threw him against his flight chair. As they shot forward out of the way of the viper-ship, he whooped with exhilaration. 'We've got a clear run at the Extractor,' he shouted.

Diesel laughed. 'Those stupid Meigwors don't even know we're here.'

'Thirty seconds,' Selene said.

Peri pushed the Nav-wheel down,

hurtling towards the surface of the Extractor. Its armour-plating was so black it was hard to see where he was flying. Peri activated ARAP – the Augmented-Reality Attack Program. The computer traced green lines over his view of the Extractor's hull so he could see the antennae and observation towers jutting from the surface. A line of red glowing spots appeared, guiding him to the ventilation shaft. He skimmed towards it, dodging radar dishes and deep-space waste chutes.

'Twelve seconds,' Selene warned. 'Eleven . . . ten . . .'

'Preparing to dislodge vent cover,' shouted Peri. 'Firing sonic pulse . . . Now!'

The shockwave blasted the vent panel into space. Peri's pod wobbled from the explosion, but he wrestled the Nav-wheel to keep it steady.

'Five seconds . . . four . . . three . . .'

Peri hit the hyper-brakes. The pod curved around into the ventilation shaft like the winning goal in a spaceball game. But the shaft was shorter than he imagined. There was barely enough room for all the pods before it narrowed into smaller ventilation ducts. 'Emergency brakes!' he screamed.

Peri slammed into his astro-harness as the pod halted an atom's breadth from the end of the main ventilation compartment. Diesel, Selene and Prince Onix followed a nanosecond behind him. Otto's pod had just cleared the opening when the computer announced, 'Cloak failure.'

'We made it!' Peri gasped over the radio, releasing his astro-harness. 'The Meigwors mustn't discover we're here, so we need to be quiet, super-stealthy!'

'The Meigwors are always stealthy!' Otto's voice growled back.

'Let's go!' Peri said and pressed his hand against the wall of his. A silver light spun around the inside surface, then the pod cracked in half.

Hiiiissssss. Two things hit Peri as the pod opened. First, a wave of noise flooded his ears – machinery thumped angrily as turbines whined and rattled. Above the sound of clashing metal, the tannoy blared computerised commands and warnings. Second, a foul stench assaulted his nose. The hot damp air reeked of rotten, nasty animal odours.

The other pods all began to crack. The *Phoenix* crew exited them and huddled around Peri. Diesel slipped a wad of Eterni-chew up his nose to block out the smell. 'What was that about making no noise?'

Diesel shouted. 'We could have a space-rock concert and no one would hear us!'

Peri led the crew down one of the smaller ventilation shafts. It was a circular tunnel made from overlapping segments of a strange pink and silver metal. The walls were covered in a thick layer of dust and grime.

'What is this stuff?' he asked.

Selene pulled a scanner from her belt and aimed it at the wall. 'Meigwor skin cells, crushed bugs and . . .' Selene dry-heaved as she hastily put the scanner away. 'You don't want to know what else.'

As they moved further down the ventilation duct, the shafts got narrower and narrower. Otto was the first to have to crawl on his hands and knees, but soon everyone was shuffling through the grime. Ahead, light streamed through the narrow slits of a vent cover in the shaft floor. Peri peered down between the gaps into a dimly lit corridor. He signalled to the others to stop. 'I'll see if the coast is clear,' he said.

Selene passed him a Swizaser and Peri vaporised the rivets around the cover. He pushed the cover aside and ducked his head down.

The stench was almost unbearable. The long circular corridor was dingy and hot. It was big enough for four Meigwors to walk side by side, but it was also filthy. The walls were blackened with slime. Strands of a glow-in-the-dark green moss hung everywhere with tiny little crab-like creatures clinging to its surface. Their glowing red eyes added to the corridor's eeriness. But there was no sign of any Meigwor soldiers or guards.

'All clear,' Peri said, stuffing a wad of Eterni-chew in his mouth. It did nothing to hide the reek as he jumped down into the corridor, brushing past the thick strands of rotting moss. His boots crunched unpleasantly as he landed on the bugs feeding off the dirt.

He took up the cosmic-combat position and watched the corridor for Meigwor guards. The others dropped down one by one. Otto was last. He stretched and twisted, then took a deep breath. 'Ah!' he boomed, 'Fresh air!'

'Which way, Otto?' Peri asked.

Otto splayed his elbows out in a Meigwor shrug. 'The vipers have reconfigured themselves to create the Extractor, but I'm not sure how they all fit together.'

'Let's keep moving,' Peri said. 'Otto, scout ahead. Diesel, follow up at the rear.'

Peri went after Otto. They kept as close to the walls as they dared, but the small crabs living in the moss snapped their claws at them if they got too close. It was slow going, waiting at the end of every corridor while Otto went ahead to stop them stumbling across a battalion of Meigwor guards.

'This way,' Otto said. 'Quick! There are guards coming from the other direction.'

Halfway down the corridor, they found a large rectangular box. Masses of bugs swarmed inside and batted against the clear windows. Otto licked his lips.

'What the *prrrip'chiq* is that?' Diesel gasped.

'A bug-o-matic!' Otto replied. 'Our brave warriors need fresh bugs! You can't fight on more than one empty stomach!'

'Gross,' Diesel muttered.

'Look!' hissed Selene, before Otto could respond to Diesel's taunt.

On the wall beside the bug-o-matic was a large touch-screen map of the Extractor.

Peri's fingers darted over it, scrolling the map one way, then another. It was covered in bizarre symbols and strange pictograms. None of it made sense.

'Otto, I need a little translation,' Peri said, pointing to the map.

'We're here,' Otto said, pointing to a symbol. 'Sector ß-õ-8-ð-Þ.'

'Hurry up,' Diesel said, motioning down the corridor towards the sound of insects being trampled. *Crunch, crunch, crunch.* 'We're going to have company.'

'The control room is located three sectors over,' Otto said, pointing to the nerve centre.

Peri traced the route across the Extractor. 'It shouldn't be too hard to get to.'

The *crunch, crunch, crunch,* was getting louder. At least three guards were heading their way!

'Come on!' Peri ordered. They raced away from the approaching guards, turning blindly around one corner and then the next. 'We need to turn left at the junction.'

'No, we need to turn right,' Otto boomed. He was about to say something else, when a strange noise echoed down the tunnel.

Clunk. Clunk-Clunk. Clunk-Clunk-beep-beep-whoooo-beep.

'Peri!' Diesel screamed.

Peri spun around and gasped. Plodding across the ceiling towards them were two gigantic crab-like robot-guards. The crab-bots had two clawed arms that swung down in front of their six metallic legs and gripped massive laserpulses. At the end of five antennae dangled the robot's illuminated eyes. They swept purple beams of light across the corridor ahead of them. Peri didn't want to find out what happened when the beams finally saw something that shouldn't have been there.

'W-w-what d-d-do we do n-n-now?' Prince Onix stuttered.

'Isn't it obvious?' Peri said. 'Run!'

Chapter 4

Clank-clank-clank.

The crab-bots scuttled after them, their metallic feet pounding against the ceiling.

Zap-Zap-Ssssizzz. Zap-Zap-Ssssizzz. Laserfire snapped at Peri's heels like Martian piranha-rats.

'Activate your Expedition Wear armour!' Peri yelled, jabbing a button on the belt of his suit. The surface instantly became hard and shiny. A Plexiglas helmet encased his head in a transparent bubble. He was just in time as a laser blast punched the back of his suit throwing him forward. Otto pulled him up.

'Keep going!' Peri yelled as a shot zinged off his helmet and exploded ahead of him. He knew their armour couldn't protect them for ever. When he saw a split up ahead in the dingy corridor, he shouted, 'Everyone go right!'

They tore around the corner into a junction between six corridors. 'Quick, this way,' said Peri, choosing one at random. There was no time to lose. 'We keep turning until we lose them.'

'That's crazy!' Otto boomed, before another blast lit the corridor behind them.

'No time to argue,' Peri panted and started running. They hung another left, twisting and changing directions wherever there was a turning.

'We've lost them,' Selene wheezed. 'I think.'

Peri skidded to a halt. He listened but couldn't hear the crab-bots' metallic feet against the ceiling.

Diesel's hair was bristling and his face was as red as a solar-flare. 'Stop being such a lamizoid, Peri. We should stop and fight.'

'If we did, they'll raise the alarm and then . . .' Peri started, but before he even finished his sentence the crab-bots were screaming, 'In-troo-Dah! In-troo-DAH!' over the ship's tannoy systems.

An alarm sounded. *Eeeee-raaaa, eeee-raaaa!*

'In-troo-Dah Alert!'

'Now the Meigwors know we're here too!' Diesel swore. 'I told you we should have blasted those crab-bots while we had the chance.'

'No more running like Milky Way

minnies!' Otto said. 'We lie in wait – like mighty Meigwors!'

He jabbed a finger into the corridor wall. A door swung out, revealing a strange kind of storeroom filled with shelves and crates. Peri glanced back down the corridor; no one was in sight yet, but it wouldn't be long before the place was crawling with guards, both Meigwor and robotic. 'Quick, inside!'

Otto flicked a switch as he pushed the door shut behind them.

'*Klûu'ah*,' Diesel exclaimed, as a bright light came on. 'Look at all these weapons.'

Peri had never seen so many weapons in his life. The wall nearest the door was covered in racks of electromagnetic zapsters, seventeen-barrelled blasters and laserpulses. There were four sets of shelves, each packed with cases of ammo and more weapons, from jellifiers to petrifiers.

Otto had brought them to the Meigwor armoury.

Selene slid out a drawer from under the jellifiers. Rows of silver probes, lasers, space-wrenches and ultra-sonic pliers gleamed back. She grabbed a few tools, tucked them in her Expedition Wear and hastily shut the drawer. 'You can never be too prepared,' she said.

Prince Onix was standing in front of a row of diagrams pasted to the wall. The posters showed the best ways to terminate a range of alien species, while others had cooking instructions. He stared at the diagram of a Xion as though hypnotised. 'Best slow roasted?' he murmured.

'Very tasty,' Otto grunted back. He was swapping his two blasters for what looked like newer, bigger versions of the same weapon.

'Otto,' Peri said, 'how come this room wasn't locked? It's full of deadly weapons.'

Otto laughed. 'Meigwors love war! Why would we want to lock ourselves out of the armoury? It just doesn't make sense!'

Diesel picked up a laserpulse. He tested it in his hands, trying to see if he could aim with it. 'We should stock up. These are much better than the double-barrel blasters we have.'

Selene had her ear against the door, her legs shaking nervously. She stiffened and put her finger to her lips. 'Shhhh . . .'

Peri pressed his ear against the door too. Outside the room, he could hear the crab-bots getting closer. *Clank. Clank. Clank.*

Keep going, Peri thought. *Keep going.*

But the crab-bots slowed as they got nearer. *Clank. Clank . . . Clank . . . Clank.*

Even with his Expedition Wear's auto-cool function working at the max, Peri felt sweat run down the inside of his suit. He held his breath, not daring to make a noise. He glanced around. Diesel's narrow band of hair had turned bone-white. Otto had blasters in each hand. Prince Onix was backing away from the door.

Clank . . .

Peri glanced behind the prince at an ammo crate sticking out from the shelves.

Onix was heading straight for it. If he bumped into it, the noise would give them away.

'Behind you,' Peri hissed.

Onix twisted around in horror as if he was expecting to find the whole Meigwor army behind him. He knocked the crate and sent it flying.

Craaaashhhh!

Instantly, the crab-bots outside screamed: 'In-troo-DAH! In-troo-DAH! In-troo-DAH!'

Peri heard Meigwor guards pounding down the corridor. He swore silently to himself. There was no way out of the armoury without a fight, which meant they had no chance of reaching the nerve centre undetected.

'Where are the intruders?' a guard boomed.

'Arr-MORE-ree,' the crab-bots screeched. 'OH-pen DOOR! WEE Diss-TROY!"

'Stupid machine! *We* destroy! Get out of the way!' the guard ordered. 'We haven't had the chance to shoot anything for ages!'

The crab-bots clunked away from the door. Fear crackled through Peri's circuits. *Once the guards open the door,* he thought, *we have a zero per cent chance of surviving and a hundred per cent chance of being blown to pieces.*

'What are we going to do?' Prince Onix whined.

Diesel grabbed a Meigwor weapon and started flicking switches along the side. 'I'm going to lock and load,' he hissed. 'We should fight our way out!'

Otto snatched the weapon from Diesel with one hand and, with the other, pushed him into the corner. Before anyone could react, he pushed Peri, Selene and Onix next

to their half-Martian friend. Otto raised the weapon at them and ran a finger across his sinewy neck.

'Step back!' he growled under his breath.

Peri's body turned ice-cold. How could he have been so stupid? He had even persuaded Otto to come along on the mission, and now the Meigwor was planning to betray them.

Chapter 5

Otto shoved Peri backwards with the tip of his blaster and reached for the door handle. As he opened the door, he swept Peri, Diesel, Selene and Onix against the wall.

Double-crossing long-necked freak! Peri cursed silently. *Bounty hunters never change.*

Selene shook Peri and pointed to her eyes, then to the door. It was blocking their view. They couldn't see the guards or the crab-bots — which meant the guards couldn't see the crew of the *Phoenix* either. They still had a chance to do something.

Selene pulled a small laser from the belt of her suit and pressed it against the open door. She fired. There was a faint whiff of vaporised metal. As the smoke cleared it left behind a perfect peephole.

Peri peered through the hole as Otto slapped his hands over his head in salute. Compared to Otto, the two guards were short and stocky, although still taller than Peri. The guards levelled their blasters at Otto. *Charrrruupt!* The sound of a laser blaster charging up sent a chill through Peri's circuits.

'What are you doing?' one of the guards boomed.

There was a long silence. Peri's heart was pounding so loudly he feared the Meigwor guards would hear it.

'I wasn't happy with my weapon!' Otto boomed. 'I wanted a bigger one that could do more damage!'

It was the first time in his life Peri had been so happy to hear someone tell a lie. Otto wasn't betraying them after all!

'With big weapons, we will all be victorious today,' the guard replied, although he didn't sound pleased. 'Not that we will need them with the Extractor working.'

'Cheer up!' replied the other. 'We're hunting intruders! If we capture them, we can slow roast them and pickle their fingers!'

Peri looked at Diesel. Blue sweat had plastered his narrow band of hair against his head. Prince Onix was keeping silent. But there was no way to hide his nerves – with each bead of sweat came a strong fishy stench.

Surely the Meigwors would smell him soon.

'Don't let me delay you!' boomed Otto.

'Go ahead! I'll grab some kit and join you soon!'

'Hold it!' the other guard shouted. 'The more I think about what you said, the more I realise . . .'

Oh no, thought Peri, pressing his eye to the door, *they don't believe Otto.*

'What?' Otto demanded.

'I wouldn't want an intruder to laugh at my blaster being so small!' the guard said. 'I need a bigger one!'

The guard stepped forward to come into the armoury, but Otto stepped in front of him. 'No!' Otto shouted at the puzzled guard. 'Take my blaster! Get after those intruders!'

'Good thinking!' The guard snatched the blaster from Otto's hand and licked his lipless mouth. 'All that talk of pickled fingers is making me hungry! We're going to eat well tonight! Come on, this way!' he shouted, leading the crab-bots away.

The *clank-clank-clank* faded as Otto closed the door.

'Wait until they've gone, space-monkeys! Then we go!' Otto growled.

'That was close,' Diesel said. 'I thought for a second you were going to give us away.'

Otto made a strange noise in the back of his throat, like a strangulated cough. It sounded deeply uncomfortable. The lumps on his throat twitched. 'Never mention it again!' he boomed. 'You may not be so lucky next time!'

Peri gulped. It must have been difficult for Otto to betray his own people. He changed the subject before Otto reconsidered. 'Otto's right. We won't be so lucky next time. Diesel, we'll need more weapons to make sure we can defend ourselves. Otto can help.'

Diesel looked like a kid in a sweet shop. His band of hair fluttered with excitement, flickering electric blue as he grabbed the nearest metallic crate from the shelves. It was a case of zirconium grenades. But as he opened it, Otto pushed him aside and started stuffing them into his Expedition Wear.

'Hey! I found them first,' Diesel objected, reaching for them.

Otto swatted him away. 'I need to restock! Worry about the others!'

Diesel's eyes flashed yellow, but he snatched a different case and unbolted it. He found a set of weapons in snug grey foam. They looked like snakes, curled ready to attack. He pulled one out and examined it in his hands.

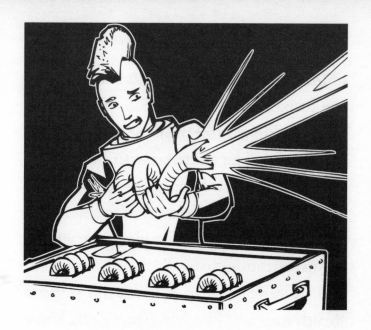

Suddenly, to Diesel's surprise, the top of the weapon lurched forward like a cobra, spitting out a fierce tongue of laserfire.

Shhhaaablam! It exploded centimetres from Otto's backside.

Otto spun round. 'Watch it!' he boomed as the black patches around his eyes darkened and he reached for a weapon on his belt.

'It was the blaster,' Diesel said, his hands shaking. 'It malfunctioned!'

Otto took the blaster from Diesel's hand and looked at it. 'Stupid space-monkey!' he said. 'Nothing wrong with this blaster! But good choice! They're perfect for our mission!'

Diesel took the cobra-shaped blaster back and handed the others to Selene, Onix and Peri. 'We're ready to blast our way to the nerve centre!'

Peri shook his head. 'Diesel, this is still a stealth mission. The Meigwors don't know where we are — let's keep it that way. We need to get to the nerve centre and shut down the Extractor quietly.'

Diesel strapped his blaster to his belt. 'I'm a hundred times stealthier than any of you!' he shouted.

Peri sighed. 'Come on, let's go — before Diesel gets any stealthier.'

Otto and Peri slipped out into the corridor first. Otto slouched ahead to make sure the next turn was clear. Selene and Onix followed, with Diesel following at the rear. They ran through the dimly lit corridors, their space boots cushioned by the moss and debris littering the floor. As they skidded into a seven-corridor junction, Peri hesitated. He racked his brains trying to recall the route he thought he'd memorised.

Clank. Clank. Clank.

'Hurry up, Peri,' Prince Onix urged. 'I hear crab-bots coming.'

'Down here,' Peri said, praying his instincts were right.

They were either running straight towards the nerve centre, or they were about to burst into a dining hall full of heavily armed, battle-hungry Meigwors.

Chapter 6

They stumbled into a section of corridor free of moss and Peri almost cheered! They were definitely heading in the right direction. The touch-screen map of the Extractor had shown the control centre surrounded by a 'clean' zone – although the Meigwors had a strange definition of 'clean'. Despite the lack of moss, crabs or beetles, the walls were still grimy. Panels in the ceiling struggled to light the corridor through layers of dirt.

Peri noticed a short corridor off to the

right and hid around the corner. 'We're close,' he panted. 'We need a plan. The nerve centre will be well guarded.'

'How about,' Diesel said, 'we go in, weapons blazing?'

Selene shot him a withering look. 'Even if we did that, we still need to know what we're up against.'

'Selene's right,' Peri said. 'We need to scout ahead.'

'Why don't we use the air vents?' Selene asked, pointing to a slatted panel above their heads. 'They're all connected to each other. It shouldn't take long to find the nerve centre and see what's what.'

'Great idea,' Peri said. 'Diesel, help me boost her up.'

'Wait! I didn't mean me!' Selene exclaimed.

'You're smallest.' Diesel grinned as he grabbed one of her feet and helped Peri lift

her up. Using the space-wrench she'd nabbed from the armoury, Selene removed the panel and handed it to Otto. She shone a torch down the duct and grimaced.

'I get all the dirty jobs,' she murmured, before sliding down the service duct. It must have been a tight fit as her elbows and knees made soft clanging sounds against the metal sides. It faded, then the noises returned. Moments later, Selene's boots came into view and she crawled out of the duct, dusting herself down.

'It's going to be harder than teaching Diesel table manners,' she said. 'The only way into the nerve centre is guarded by a big, ugly Meigwor who has a whole armoury on his back. The door is locked. The vent is welded shut. But the three technicians in the nerve centre appeared to be unarmed.'

'Maybe Otto could get close enough to the guard without raising the alarm and disable him,' Peri said. 'Then we can blast the door and overpower the controllers.'

'I have a better idea, space-monkeys!' Otto grinned as he pulled his blaster from his snakeskin belt. He aimed it at them. 'Hands up! I take you as prisoners!'

A cold shiver crackled through Peri's circuits. Diesel shouted, 'I knew we shouldn't trust him!' He started to raise his own weapon, but Selene stood in front of him.

'Lamizoid!' Selene said. 'Otto only wants to *pretend* he's captured us – so we can over-power the guard and controllers together. Isn't that right?'

'That's what I said!' Otto boomed. 'I tackle the guard, you storm the controllers!'

Peri nodded, but he was going to make

sure he and Diesel were at the front with their weapons tucked behind their backs just in case.

With their hands up, Otto marched them down the corridor to the brightly lit area outside the nerve centre. Peri held his breath. The guard, as massive as Otto, charged up his electromagnetic zapster and barked, 'Halt!'

'I have prisoners to eject out of the airlock!' Otto boomed.

The guard laughed. 'Well done, but this isn't an airlock!' He pointed to the door behind him. 'Only the controllers can open this!'

'My mistake!' Otto boomed as he clapped his hands over his head. 'Long live Meigwor!'

As the guard returned the salute, Otto punched him. *Smaccckkk.* The guard staggered backwards.

Clllaaannng! The guard slammed into the nerve-centre door.

Shhuuuh! The door slid open. 'Keep it down out there!' A Meigwor controller stood in the doorway. 'What the . . .' he boomed, seeing the unconscious guard on the ground.

Diesel stuck his blaster in the controller's face. 'Don't move!'

'Let's go!' shouted Peri as he rushed into the nerve centre. Onix and Selene tackled the nearest controller, who had his hand stuck in a bug-o-matic.

Peri aimed his blaster at the others. 'Step away from the equipment,' he ordered.

The controllers were short by Meigwor standards. Peri guessed that they had no combat training – they didn't even try to fight.

'Move over there.' Peri pointed towards the door.

Peri looked around the nerve centre. The room was filled with buzzing and beeping. Lights flashed across four different control consoles. Monitors covered every centimetre of the walls, and a massive plasma screen hung in the centre of the room. Peri could see more viper-ships joining the Extractor, more tentacles flying out to suck the life from Xion, and more images of the planet's people suffocating in the dusty streets.

'We've got to seal the door and work out how to disable the Extractor,' Peri shouted.

Otto grabbed the controllers and tossed them out before slamming the door shut. 'We must prepare for a counter-attack,' he boomed. 'Help me push this bug-o-matic in front of the door.'

'Diesel, Onix,' Peri said, 'you two help

Otto. Selene and I will figure out how to destroy the Extractor.'

As the others took up defensive positions, Peri and Selene studied the Extractor's controls. But neither of them knew where to start. Selene turned a couple of dials hopefully.

Nothing happened.

Peri hoped his bionic half might know what to do, but he felt no connection with this alien ship.

'It's no good,' Peri said. 'It's going to take for ever to work out what half these controls do!'

Bang-Bang-Bang! Explosions shook the door.

'Hurry up,' Diesel shouted. 'It won't hold for long!'

'We're trying,' Peri yelled, flicking a series of zip-dials. 'We need a short cut!'

'That's it,' Selene said. 'Not a shortcut, but a short circuit!'

Peri nodded. 'Great idea.' He slid under the main control console and ripped off an access panel. He grabbed the tangle of wires with his fist and yanked them out, shielding his face as hot sparks exploded around him.

He heard Selene sigh. 'Nothing's happening.'

'Hold it,' Peri said, sliding his head out from under the console. 'Maybe I can overload the system, rather than pull it apart?'

'But that would need another source of power,' she replied.

'I'm half bionic – I can use my internal batteries as a counter-charge!' Peri exclaimed.

'That could kill you!' she gasped.

'There's no other choice.' Peri grabbed

67

two wires. As they touched together, they sparked.

He took a deep breath, then pushed the wires into his forearm. He gritted his teeth against the pain as he forced them through his nerves and muscles to the circuits underneath. Something like plasma-lightning flashed through him, making his limbs spasm and his circuits burn. It was like fire ripping through his skin.

Alien computer code stormed his head. There was so much information, Peri could feel his brain heating up. He imagined melting grey matter dripping from his ears.

'I'm not giving up without a fight!' he muttered as he pushed back against the assault with his mind.

Kaboom! The door to the control room exploded, followed by a dozen smoke grenades.

'Hurry up, Peri,' Diesel shouted. 'We've got company!'

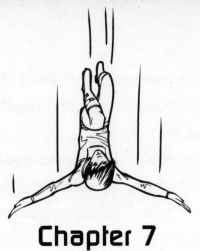

Chapter 7

As the smoke cleared, laserfire lit up the nerve centre. *Zap-blam-blam-sssizzz!*

Pulses of green and red pinged back and forth between the crew and the guards. The bug-o-matic prevented the guards storming further into the room than the doorway. Otto had a blaster in each hand and wasn't even bothering to take cover. He faced the guards, dodging the zapster fire as the monitors exploded behind him.

'Otto, use a flash grenade,' Diesel shouted.

The bounty hunter flung a grenade from

his belt at the Meigwor guards. *Kaaa-boom!*
A bright light exploded, temporarily blind-ing them.

In the lull, Diesel sprinted towards
Selene. The engineer crouched down with
her hands linked together ready to lift him
into the air. As he stepped on to her hands,
she boosted him upwards. Diesel somer-saulted across the room. He grabbed hold

of the main monitor hanging in the middle and climbed on to it. Then he opened fire with his blaster.

As the Meigwor guards ducked, Selene rolled towards Onix. The Xion prince had built a barrier in front of Peri's console made from pieces of computers, melted technicians' chairs and charred manuals. Once she was safely behind the barricade, Diesel backflipped from his hanging perch and landed in a perfect crouch behind the chairs. He threw himself against the barrier and unleashed another round of blaster fire.

'*Mars 'rakk!*' Diesel taunted. 'Is that all you got? I had better aim when I was a baby!'

The console behind Peri took a direct hit, showering him with molten sparks. It didn't matter. He had to ignore what was happening in the control centre. His battle was with the Extractor itself. He used his bionic senses to weave through the Meigwor computer code. By mentally ducking and diving, sneaking and sliding, he navigated the alien system, searching for the main control functions.

But it knew he was there, and sent a surge of power to blast him away from the Extractor's core. It swamped his mind with thousands of small computer codes and programs, making every nerve and circuit in his head feel as though it had been dipped in molten metal. The pain screamed at him to disconnect himself, but Peri kept dodging and twisting through the surge.

He caught glimpses of the Extractor's own camera feeds, showing him the battle in the nerve centre from every angle. He didn't understand how his bionic brain could hold so many images and information in one split second. He could see Onix firing wildly at the Meigwor guards. Selene and Diesel were shooting with extreme accuracy. He wanted to help his friends, but he had a fight of his own to finish first.

The Extractor dashed him away from the camera feeds, plunging him deeper and deeper into the program until it felt as though he was drowning in computer code. It kept crashing against his mind with blocks of data, rolling his brain around in a storm of alien symbols.

He was disorientated. He didn't know where he was or how far he was from the core program. He pushed hard against it and surfaced back in his body. He took a deep breath then dived again into the Extractor with his mind. It pushed Peri back. The computer slammed everything it had into his body. Every nerve and wire inside him was under assault. His skin crackled with a white-hot web of electricity, each spark stinging him like a Martian-wasp. He had to pull the wires from his arm soon, or he was going to explode!

Kaaaa-boooom! Another grenade rattled the nerve centre. Diesel slammed against the console above him. The gunner's Expedition Wear was in shreds. Peri looked down, seeing Selene and Onix pressed against the barricade. Wisps of smoke rose from their smouldering suits. He had to help his crew! Peri grabbed the wires to pull them out, but hesitated.

What am I doing? he asked himself. His friends were still fighting, risking their lives to help the dying Xion people. Millions of lives and an entire galaxy were at stake. It didn't matter if all Peri's circuits were fried.

The Meigwors *had* to be stopped.

Peri let go of the wires and traced the power throbbing through his circuits. The Extractor was trying to saturate his body with electricity. But instead of frying his circuits, he realised it was giving him greater power! The more energy that flowed into him, the stronger a weapon he became. All he had to do now was turn the power-flow in the opposite direction, back into the Extractor.

Starting at his feet, he reversed the current. He pushed a cosmic-wave of destruction through his body, adding as much of his own energy as he could. It coursed through him like a fireball before bursting from him. Every megawatt of power he could find flowed into the Extractor. He raced it towards the core, making it pick up more energy as it did.

Krrraaccckkk-BLLLAAAAAMMMMM!

The console exploded, throwing Peri backwards into the air and ripping the wires from his skin. His bionic self instantly took control of his muscles, turning him in a twisting somersault. He landed

safely next to Diesel and he grabbed a spare weapon from the half-Martian's holster and started firing.

'Glad you could join us,' Diesel said.

Peri, Onix, Selene and Diesel ducked more shots from the Meigwor guards. Molten plastic sprayed up from the chairs. There was no way to escape now – they had no choice but to fight, and hope that they survived.

'For the Milky Way!' Peri shouted.

The ship shuddered as though there was a spacequake and the laserfire stopped.

Raaaa-eeee! Raaa-eeee! Raaa-eee! Sirens blared as an electronic voice screamed, 'Extractor dismantling! Emergency! Emergency!'

The Meigwor guards dropped their weapons and dashed into the corridor and out of sight.

'What's happening?' Selene shouted.

Otto edged around the barricade to look at the only undamaged monitor. 'The Extractor's breaking up into separate viper-ships again!' he boomed. 'We've done it!'

'Time to get out of here,' Peri shouted.

They pushed through the throng of panicked Meigwors. But it wasn't the clean escape they hoped for. A new battalion of guards appeared in the corridor ahead, pounding towards them with their weapons blazing.

Diesel set his blaster to Continuous Pulse and opened fire, but his aim was thrown by another shudder rocking the Extractor. His laser melted a small hole in the deck.

'Fire at the floor,' the gunner barked. 'Continuous Pulse!'

Peri and Otto joined him in firing at the same spot. The three beams made the floor dissolve like a sun going supernova. Before the Meigwor guards had time to do more than scream, the floor simply melted away and sent them tumbling down a huge hole in the deck.

They had no time to cheer. Yet another explosion shook the Extractor. They slipped along a narrow ledge around the hole and then sprinted down the corridor.

'Which way?' Selene asked at the junction.

Instantly, Peri could see the layout of the whole ship in his mind's eye. It took only nanoseconds to see the best route back to the mini-pods. He couldn't believe it. During his fight with the Extractor, he must have absorbed the design of the whole vessel.

'This way!' he shouted.

They raced as fast as they could. It didn't matter about the guards. They just had to make it back to the pods before the Extractor dismantled or exploded. Peri rounded the corner and saw two crab-bots hanging from the ceiling.

The robot-guards barely had time to say 'In-troo-DAH!' before he, Diesel, Selene, Otto and Onix blasted them into a gazillion smoking fragments.

'Keep going,' Peri shouted, racing down another corridor. The vent hatch was still open. Otto boosted him and the others into the shaft and climbed up last. It was still hot and cramped in the ventilation shaft, but it didn't matter. They crawled as fast as they could towards the pods. They could hear the shouts of the Meigwor guards following behind them, 'Take them dead or alive! For Meigwor!'

Peri was the first out of the ventilation shaft to where the mini-pods were waiting.

'Otto, you were the last one in, go!' he ordered. 'You next, Onix, then Diesel, and Selene.'

Peri crouched by the shaft and fired his blaster towards the attacking Meigwors to buy his friends some more time. One by one, the mini-pods sealed themselves and then shot off into space. Now, it was Peri's turn. He knew as soon as he stopped firing he wouldn't have long to escape. He counted under his breath, 'Three, two, one!' Then he dropped his weapon and leapt into his mini-pod. It sealed around him as he engaged the thrusters.

But even at bionic speed, he wasn't fast enough. As Peri cleared the vent, he saw the Meigwor guards reach the narrow chamber and open fire.

Baaammm! A blast shuddered through the mini-pod.

Chapter 8

Peri's mini-pod spun away from the Extractor. He jammed the Nav-wheel left and right. Nothing. He tried firing the manoeuvring thrusters and slamming on the hyper-brakes. Nothing worked. The Meigwor guards had scored a direct hit as he tried to escape. The pod's controls were wrecked. He could see the other mini-pods heading for the *Phoenix* and tried to radio for help, but that was dead too.

'Pod engine failing!' announced the pod's computer. 'Fuel leakage catastrophic.'

'No!' Peri hit the control panel. The guard's shots had wiped out the engines and fuel-cells too.

He stared at the chaos outside, helpless to do anything. The Extractor was retracting its tentacles from the now wrinkled atmosphere of Xion, leaving clouds of orange dust trailing through space. At the same time, viper-ships were breaking away from the weapon. The tentacles smashed into the ships, destroying some and flinging huge chunks of debris out into space.

Peri gasped as a massive ragged piece of shielding blazed within a hair's breadth of his pod. Any closer, it would have smashed him to smithereens. But without engines or life support, he wouldn't last for long.

No, no, no, he thought, *this can't be the end.*

'Help!' he screamed. 'He . . . lp . . .'

Peri couldn't breathe. The oxygen monitor had dropped to less than five per cent. The emergency console lights dimmed. The power reserves were falling fast. The pod was getting colder. He closed his eyes, trying to shut out the sickening ache in his stomach, and recited the words he'd heard General Pegg use on the IF Remembrance Day. 'Those born of stardust are destined to return to it. We honour the brave who die knowing they will not see the better world they strived for . . .'

The pod stopped spinning. Peri felt a flicker of hope and opened his eyes. His view was blocked by a strange, orange light that rippled and writhed round his pod – a lasernet!

The Phoenix *must have heard my call,* Peri thought, as the net dragged the mini-pod back to the great ship.

The lights blacked out.

Clunk! Whiiirrr.

Peri's chair dropped away, sending him sliding down a long docking tube and out on to the Bridge.

'Thank you, *Phoenix*!' he whooped.

Selene gave him a high five. 'The *Phoenix* shot out a web to catch your pod and brought you back – amazing!'

Even Diesel had a relieved grin on his face. But before he could say a word, the Bridge was lit by an explosion on the 360-monitor. *Kaaaboooomm!*

The Extractor had erupted into a gazillion pieces. Chunks of burning wreckage were flung in every direction, forcing the surviving viper-ships to blast anything that got in their way.

Peri punched the air. The Extractor was no more.

'Let's hope that my planet won't be able to build another one for a hundred years!' Otto said, sombrely. 'Xion is safe!'

'Look,' Prince Onix exclaimed, pointing at the 360-monitor. Xion fighters were blasting through the holes in the Cos-Moat, firing cluster missiles at the retreating viper-ships.

'Incoming message,' the *Phoenix* announced as the King of Xion appeared in the middle of the monitor.

'Thank you for saving Xion!' the king cheered.

'Don't forget our deal, Your Majesty,' Peri replied. 'You promised never to attack the Milky Way again. And, you said you'd send us home.'

'Of course,' the king said. 'I'll create another vortex just like the one you *destroyed*.'

'Just like the one you used to *attack* our galaxy,' Diesel replied.

The gunner's eyes were flashing yellow. It wasn't easy to forget that the Xion had blown up the IF Station. Since the Xion vortex sucked the *Phoenix* into the Ubi galaxy, they had had no contact with their home.

They didn't even know if there still *was* a Milky Way to return to.

'The past can't be changed,' the king replied. 'But I am sorry.' He looked away from the camera. 'Create the vortex!'

'Yes!' Prince Onix exclaimed. 'I've always wanted to see the Milky Way!'

The king slammed his fist down. 'You will return to your official duties, my son.'

'But I want to stay with my friends!' Onix howled.

'You are the heir to the throne of Xion,' the king said. 'Now you must start to behave like it!'

'But I don't want to be king. I want to be a Star Fighter.'

The blood vessels on the king's face bulged as if they were about to explode. Onix looked around for support from his friends. He shot Selene a smile, but the engineer just rolled her eyes.

The king said nothing. But Peri noticed him nod as if someone was talking to him off-screen. His eyes flicked back to Peri.

'The vortex is ready. Good luck, Earthlings!' the king said before he vanished from the monitor.

Peri couldn't believe it. After all this time, they were finally going home! Peri sat in the captain's chair and an astro-harness snaked around him as the churning centre of the vortex rapidly expanded in front of them.

Peri's mouth felt dry. A vortex was one of the deadliest things in the universe. Even with the excitement of going home, he knew it wasn't over yet. As the vortex spiralled outwards, debris and damaged ships were sucked into it. They exploded into huge multi-coloured blooms of fire as the awesome astronomical forces ripped them apart.

'Strap in,' Peri ordered. 'Selene, stand by to engage Superluminal speed.'

Selene reached for the red touchpad, ready to activate the controls. The *Phoenix* slid towards the vortex, getting faster and faster as the gravitational pull got stronger.

'Everyone's going to be so relieved when I return,' Diesel said. 'There will be the biggest celebration ever! I can't wait to tell them how I foiled a Meigwor plot, saved the moon-bats, fought the Xio-Bot, blew up the Extractor *and* got Xion to stop attacking the Milky Way! I'm going to be the biggest hero ever!'

Selene cleared her throat and glared at him.

'I'll make sure someone gives you guys a medal or something,' Diesel replied. 'They always listen to my recommendations.'

An alarm sounded. 'Intruder alert!' the *Phoenix* warned.

Before Peri could even check the sensors, Prince Onix started yelling, 'No!' Peri twisted around in his chair. The Xion General Dachkor had an arm wrapped around the prince. 'Let go of me!'

'What's the meaning of this?' Peri shouted.

'King's orders!' replied the general, pressing the bright orange teleportation device strapped to his wrist.

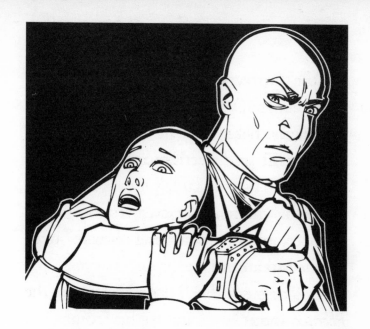

'*Noooooooo!*' Onix screamed before he and the general winked out of existence.

Another alarm sounded. *Eeee-raaa! Eeee-raaa!*

'Behind us,' Diesel shouted.

Peri looked. A Meigwor viper-ship had used sonic-grapplers to hold on to the rear of the *Phoenix*.

Selene checked some calculations on the monitor. 'We can't blast it off from this range.'

'Don't worry, we'll lose them when we go Superluminal,' Peri replied. But he could see Selene shaking her head.

'We can't go Superluminal with a viper attached to us!' she said. 'Our engines aren't powerful enough. We have to break the connection! Circle around before we're crushed to atoms!'

Peri twisted the Nav-wheel, but the *Phoenix* didn't respond to his command. 'It's no good,' he cried. 'The vortex is too strong!'

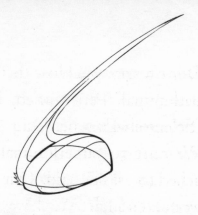

Chapter 9

Space currents rocked the Bridge as the *Phoenix* looped the outermost rim of the vortex. The Velocity View showed they weren't going fast enough to escape the vortex. Unless they got rid of the viper-ship and went Superluminal soon, the vortex's currents were going to tear the ship apart.

Peri's heart pounded in time with the flashing red lights on the control panel. The computer calmly proclaimed, 'Hull integrity 62%, weakening. Five minutes to hull collapse.'

'I don't know how to get rid of them!' Selene shrieked, turning dials desperately.

'Do something!' Otto and Diesel screamed, for once in unison. A rainbow of colours flashed through Diesel's bristling band of hair.

Phoenix, Peri thought. *Help us! What should we do?*

Phhhooomph! The ship shuddered and lurched forward.

Peri glanced back. He didn't understand. The viper was gone. It had vanished without a trace. There was only one answer, the *Phoenix* had heard his cry for help!

'This ship rocks!' he whooped. 'Selene: Superluminal, please!'

'You bet!' Selene slid open the red Superluminal panel and, with a grin on her face, flicked the switches.

Nothing happened.

As Selene flicked the switches again, she started to frown. 'It's not working . . .'

Peri snapped his fingers and the control panel slid close to him. He flicked the red switches himself, but still nothing happened. 'The viper must have damaged the *Phoenix*,' he said.

'If we don't go Superluminal in under three minutes, we'll disintegrate!' Selene yelled.

Peri tried to contain his panic and looked over the controls again. He tried to ignore the spinning vortex outside, but he knew only Superluminal speed could save them. 'We're just going to have to face it . . . we're as good as dead . . .'

'That's it!' Selene exclaimed, scrambling over the control panel to the button at the very top. 'The very last page of the manual has only one instruction: *When you stare death in the face, press the Blue Helix!'* She pointed at a strange twisted button that glowed with a ghostly blue light.

'But we don't know what the Blue Helix even does!' Peri said. 'It could be the self-destruct button!'

'Do you have a better idea?' Selene asked.

Peri's circuits fizzed with fear. They had

run out of options. Pressing the Blue Helix was their last resort – the only possible way out. He nodded and Selene slammed her hand down on the blue button.

The *Phoenix* shook violently and noisily, as if the vortex was ripping it apart.

Crrrraaacccaaachhhaaa! Searing white light exploded through the Bridge, followed by an ear-splitting *BANG!*

Peri blinked. He didn't believe what he was seeing. He checked the 360-monitor and the radar screen. Then he rubbed his eyes and checked again.

It can't be, he thought. *It's not possible.*

But it was. He could see the *Phoenix* – or a ship that looked exactly like it – in the 360-monitor right in front of them. He looked around. *But I'm still on board,* he thought.

Diesel's strip of hair was every possible

colour, showing his complete confusion. 'How can there be two *Phoenixes* in the vortex now?' he said.

Peri turned to Selene. 'Are we there or here?' he asked.

'Both!' Selene said as she studied the monitor. 'It's amazing. The Blue Helix has allowed us to travel back in time, but only by 5.451 minutes. It's like a cosmic make-over button. We're here in the future and there in the past.'

'Are you crazy?' Diesel shouted. 'How is that even possible?'

'Shut up, Diesel!' Peri yelled. 'Just look!'

The *Phoenix* in front still had the Meigwor viper-ship attached to the hull.

'We're flying behind ourselves,' Peri explained. 'That's how the viper disappeared from the hull. We blasted it off ourselves by going back in time.'

'But why didn't we see ourselves behind the ship?' Diesel asked.

'Because we hadn't done it yet,' Selene said. 'We can't see our future selves in the past, only our past selves in the future.'

Otto groaned and put his head between his hands. 'Stop explaining and just shoot the viper!'

'Diesel, activate the *Phoenix*'s laser cannons,' Peri said. 'Let's get rid of that Meigwor sucker!'

'Wait,' Selene said. 'We mustn't damage ourselves in the past – nor the present or future. We need to use a vaporising laser beam. It's the only way to make sure there'll be no debris to hit us.'

There was no time to argue. The hull integrity was down to 32%.

'Diesel, stand down,' Peri said as he activated the laser controls in front of him. A target tracker whooshed from one side of his chair and a control stick from the other. He gripped the stick and started mapping the viper-ship with the targeting sensors.

'Hull integrity 17.3%,' called Selene. 'We don't have much longer!'

Peri concentrated. He had almost outlined the whole vessel with the laser array. Just a little more and he could save the Past-*Phoenix*. He just had to make sure none of the beams hit the Present-*Phoenix*. Or was it the Future-*Phoenix*? He wasn't sure.

So I'll just save them all, he thought.

'Firing now!'

Orange lasers blazed from their spaceship. They seemed to move almost in slow motion against the fierce swirling mass of the vortex, but they hit the viper-ship in an instant. The Meigwor ship glowed for a matter of seconds before it vanished in a puff of smoke!

'We've done it!' Selene exclaimed. 'Now to try Superluminal again!'

Peri flicked the red switches. Nothing.

'I don't understand!' Selene cried.

Suddenly, every circuit inside him was tingling with instructions from the *Phoenix* – in the past and the present.

He knew what they needed to do.

Peri pushed the thrusters to maximum and fired the *Phoenix*'s boosters. The ship surged forward, towards the Past-*Phoenix*.

Diesel tried to grab the controls from him. 'Have you gone mad?'

'Trust me!' Peri yelled, pushing him away from the controls. Otto grabbed Diesel and dragged him away.

'It's certain death anyway!' Otto boomed,

restraining Diesel. 'Let him try anything he wants!'

As the vortex swirled around them and the Past-*Phoenix* loomed larger on the 360-monitor, Peri adjusted the controls slightly. There was only one chance to get this right.

Another shockwave rocked the Bridge. Otto and Diesel tumbled backwards. Peri held steady, fighting every impulse to pull away. It was their only chance. They hurtled towards the Past-*Phoenix*. Its sleek white hull was so close, Peri could see it sparkling. Proximity alarms erupted across the Bridge, before the Present-*Phoenix* slammed into the back of its earlier self.

The purest white light Peri's bionic eyes had ever seen flooded the Bridge.

Chapter 10

Peri's body ached as though he had been pulled apart then stitched back together again. He remembered crashing towards the Past-*Phoenix* and then the white light.

Have I died?

He opened his eyes, finding that he was in the captain's chair. Next to him, Selene was strapped in, unconscious. Otto and Diesel were lying on the deck.

Peri's astro-harness released him. He stood up and gazed at the 360-monitor. It was the most incredible sight he had

ever seen. The vortex and the Past-*Phoenix* were gone. Instead, an enormous rainbow of galactic confetti had been smeared across space. A swirling stripe surrounded them, sparkling and glistening with every colour imaginable and then some.

Peri nudged Diesel with his foot. 'Wake up!' he shouted. 'We did it. We're alive!'

'What?' Diesel moaned as Peri pulled him up.

'The vortex didn't destroy us! We destroyed *it*! Look — all that's left is a rainbow-coloured scar!'

'You woke me for scenery?' Diesel brushed his hand through his hair. 'I don't understand. How did we survive the crash?'

'We didn't crash into another ship,' Peri said. 'We crashed into our *own* ship.'

'We crashed into ourselves?' Diesel stuck a wad of Eterni-chew in his mouth. 'That doesn't even make sense.'

'Yes it does,' said Selene. She had just woken up, but she was already checking the controls. 'Our present selves crashed into our past selves. The universe can't sustain two versions of the *Phoenix* for very long – so, when the two ships crashed together, it created a natural explosion that gave us a Superluminal boost. That dragged both versions of us, and the *Phoenix*, back into the present.'

Diesel was holding his head. 'Enough!' he growled. 'Just tell me if we're back to normal or not!'

'We are,' said Peri, feeling tingles of gratitude that, yet again, the amazing ship had saved their lives. 'And we are back in the Milky Way at last!'

Diesel and Selene cheered.

Otto had woken up and was getting to his feet. 'But that vortex was my only route back to Meigwor!'

'You're part of our crew now,' Peri said. It felt odd saying it, but he knew it was true.

'Don't remind me!' Otto boomed.

Peri, Selene and Diesel laughed. It was good to be back in their own solar system again.

'Set a course for the IF Space Sta—' Peri stopped mid-word as he remembered seeing the Xions destroy the space station during the attack on the Milky Way. 'Where should we go?'

Selene brought up a map of the solar system on the display. 'When we left, the Intergalactic Force had bases on every planet – and quite a few comets, too.'

'But which ones survived the attack?' Peri asked. 'We should head for Earth first. If it's still there.' He hesitated before he instructed the 360-monitor to zoom in on Earth. Peri held his breath as the monitor flickered and flashed, homing in on Peri's planet. Relief washed over him as the familiar blue-and-green sphere came into focus.

He smacked the pyramid-shaped button to fire up the engines. The *Phoenix* shot towards the heart of the solar system. As they swept around Mars, Diesel grinned. His hair changed to the same dusty red colour of the planet.

As Earth came into view, Peri saw that the IF Space Station was gone. Not even a speck of dust was left from the attack. Diesel's hair flopped and turned ash-white. Peri and Selene gasped.

'At least we've stopped Xion attacking again,' Selene muttered.

Peri started scanning Earth. Carbon dioxide levels were OK. Its defensive satellite seemed to be back in action.

'Incoming message from the IF,' the *Phoenix* announced.

'How are we going to explain Otto?' Diesel asked.

'You're right!' Peri exclaimed. 'We need the right moment to tell them why the Intergalactic Force now has a Meigwor in its ranks. Otto, you'd better find somewhere to hide.'

'Meigwors don't hide! We lie in wait!' he growled as he lumbered off to the nearest portal and vanished.

A com-screen whirred from the console. The screen flickered into life. A familiar man with short white hair and an IF uniform appeared. He looked worn out.

'Peace in space, General Pegg.' Peri saluted him.

'Peace in space, cadet, welcome home,' the general replied. 'The emperor thanks you for keeping his son safe.'

'Actually, sir,' Diesel interrupted. 'I was never in any danger. I'm one of the top cadets in the academy —'

'Thank you, Diaxo,' the general said briskly.

General Pegg continued: 'Peri, I'm sure you're worried about your parents. They're safe. We evacuated all technical and scientific staff from the space station before it was destroyed.'

Peri punched the air.

'The royal family is also safe,' the general went on. 'Thankfully, we're going to have to wait a long time for the reign of Diaxo Samuel Elliotte the Tenth!'

Peri couldn't help laughing – until he saw the serious look on the general's face. 'The *Phoenix* has sent across preliminary reports. You disobeyed a direct order.'

An electric shock filled Peri's stomach. Were they going to be punished?

'However, you and Diaxo have proved yourselves to be great Star Fighters. I'd like you to finish your cadet training, but, frankly, your galaxy needs you. What do you say? Are you ready for another mission, this time as full Star Fighters?'

Peri stared at General Pegg. Since being sucked through the vortex to the Ubi Galaxy, he had been desperate to go home. But now he was here, and he knew his parents were safe, what did he truly want?

Did he want to return to the cadet classroom? Or did he want to return to outer space, and all the adventures it held?

Peri glanced at Diesel. The grin on his gunner's face said it all. Peri nodded and they both turned to General Pegg. 'We'll do it!'

'As long as I'm still in charge,' Diesel added.

The general nodded. 'Dock with the Moon refuelling station. Once you've been debriefed and the *Phoenix* has been . . . ' The general suddenly stopped speaking. His face turned red with a strange mixture of horror and anger as he looked over Peri's shoulder.

'I can't believe it,' the general shouted.

Peri's body tingled with dread as he feared the general had seen Otto. He spun around, but only Selene stood behind them.

'Is that . . .' But before the general could finish his sentence, Selene pushed forward and slammed the monitor back into the control panel.

'Why did you do that?' Diesel yelled.

Selene flapped her hand as if to dismiss his question. 'Me and the general have a bit of a history. I'll tell you all about it later.'

Peri grinned. He had a feeling that, now they were real Star Fighters, their adventures were only just beginning!

Join Peri and the crew of the *Phoenix*
on their next mission!

Can Peri and the crew track down
notorious space pirate Jaxx?

Find out! In . . .

PIRATE AMBUSH

COMING SOON!

Turn over to read Chapter 1

Chapter 1

'There's no hiding, from me!' Peri flew his fighter pod tight around the curved hull of a star cruiser. His searchlight flicked across the battered surface of the ship looking for the next beacon.

Peri glanced at the countdown monitor. Only twenty minutes left. This was his final Star Fighter test – an obstacle course throughout the Milky Way. His challenge was to collect the last three beacons and make it back to base before the clock timed out. If he succeeded, he would become the youngest ever Star Fighter.

If he failed, he wouldn't get another chance.

Peri flew over a large gash in the star cruiser's hull. He didn't need the search beam to see the flashing beacon down in a tangle of twisted metal. He plunged his pod towards it. The beacon was barely bigger than a grenade. He slowed down as much as he dared and activated the transporter beam. There was a flash of light. 'Beacon beamed aboard!' the ship's computer announced.

'Eighteen down!' Peri whooped as he blasted away from the cruiser. 'Two to go!'

'Collision alert!' his ship screeched as warning lights flashed. Peri's heart pounded like a pulsar.